Spies!

A children's story by Chris Esola

Illustrations by Andrew Guerrino

Spies!

And as the story was told . . .

Matilda was a rescue puppy from Tennessee.
Matilda, her mommy, and her brothers and sisters
were abandoned by their owners.
They were all pretty sick when they were rescued.

Most people don't know this, but the place that rescued Matilda was surrounded by highly trained feline operatives.

SHHH!

They trained Matilda in combat operations.
They showed her how to be ninja-like,
and able to walk and go where
most puppies could not imagine...
like walking on ledges without being detected.

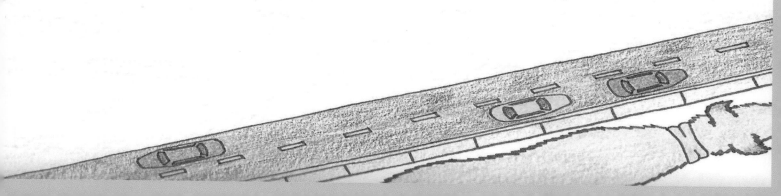

The most important thing that the feline operatives taught Matilda is how to detect spies. They told Matilda that spies are everywhere! Matilda told her family that the biggest spies are squirrels. Chipmunks are other highly trained spies. Birds are not as good at being spies, but they have a huge advantage of being able to fly.

On any given day, Matilda will bark at squirrels, chipmunks, and birds... she barks the loudest at squirrels saying "spies, look spies!"

Matilda is the best spy detector in the world and alerts everyone around.

Matilda's new family in New York is very happy
that they have a trained spy detector.
Matilda's new family calls her
their little gift from heaven.

. . . the end!